Molly Pitcher

Tale retold by Larry Dane Brimner
Illustrated by Patrick Girouard

Adviser: Dr. Alexa Sandmann, Professor of Literacy,
The University of Toledo; Member, International Reading Association

✦ COMPASS POINT BOOKS
Minneapolis, Minnesota

Compass Point Books
3109 West 50th Street, #115
Minneapolis, MN 55410

Visit Compass Point Books on the Internet at *www.compasspointbooks.com*
or e-mail your request to *custserv@compasspointbooks.com*

Dedication
To girls everywhere who are brave, strong, and independent.
-LDB

Editor: Catherine Neitge
Designer: Les Tranby

Library of Congress Cataloging-in-Publication Data
The cataloging-in-publication data is on file with the Library of Congress.
ISBN 0-7565-0604-2
2003020065

Printed in the United States of America.

Table of Contents

Preparing for War

Mary Hays, who some called Molly, looked around the Army camp at Valley Forge, Pennsylvania. The snow was deep that winter of 1777–1778. General George Washington's ragtag troops had no warm clothes and very little food. Many were sick. They looked more like worn-out ragamuffins than soldiers. In truth, most of the men in camp that night were not soldiers at all. They were shopkeepers and

4

merchants and farmers. They were used to being in forests to track and hunt deer, not an enemy army.

Like Molly's husband, William, these men were just doing their part in the fight to free the American colonies from the king of England.

Washington's men didn't know how to fight like soldiers in an open battlefield, and that's what they knew they'd soon be doing. Many of them deserted and returned home rather than go up against the well-trained British soldiers. Even so, Washington vowed to turn his remaining men into first-rate soldiers. He asked Baron Friedrich Wilhelm Augustus von Steuben to help. Baron von Steuben had been an officer in the Prussian army.

Somehow, von Steuben did what Washington asked him to do. In a matter of a few months, he turned these shopkeepers, merchants, and farmers into soldiers. Any general would have been proud to command them. When it was time for the troops to move on, William Hays was with them.

What about Molly? She walked along not far behind.

Molly wasn't alone as she trudged along with the troops. Many women and children joined their loved ones in Washington's Army—and the British Army, too. Molly and the other women took care of the sick, washed clothes, and cooked. They even joined their men on the battlefield. (But more about that later!) Some of the wives just came for short visits. Others, like Molly, stayed for months and months. Think about this: Some women and children had nowhere else to go.

Doing What She Could

That June morning of 1778 was hotter than blazes in Monmouth Courthouse, New Jersey. Some said it was as hot as a blacksmith's forge! The weather didn't stop the American troops, under the command of General Charles Lee, from firing on the British. No, siree.

With sounds of war all around her, Molly wondered how she could best help the American cause. When one of the brave soldiers went down, exhausted from the heat, she spied her old pewter pitcher. It was then that Molly knew what she could do.

As quick as a cricket, she snatched up the old pitcher and raced lickety-split to a nearby spring. She filled her pitcher full of cool water and dashed back to the fighting. Molly gave the water to the exhausted soldier. His thirst quenched, the soldier picked up his musket, loaded it, and started fighting again.

You might think that Molly returned to the safety of camp after that, but you'd be wrong. Before she'd even finished giving water to the first soldier, another one hollered, "Molly! Pitcher!" Molly did what she was asked, carrying the pitcher of water to the other soldier.

That's how it went the rest of the morning. "Molly! Pitcher!" men chorused all across the battlefield. Molly kept running, fetching water for the American soldiers.

The British marched into battle already sweating in their heavy, wool uniforms and black fur hats. As the day grew hotter, those British soldiers who weren't wounded or killed began falling left and right, like plants that had gone too long without rain. Even as they fell, however, scores of other soldiers took their places.

There were so many British soldiers, in fact, that some of the Americans began to get skittish. They deserted their positions and hightailed it to safer parts. General Lee gave the order to retreat, but those soldiers who remained on the battlefield ignored his order. They held their positions. They continued to fight, so Molly kept doing her job, too—toting water to them.

After that, everyone just naturally called her Molly Pitcher.

Molly Fights a Battle

The battle waged on in the heat of the day. Smoke and the smell of gunpowder filled the air. Nothing seemed to stop Molly. Trip after trip, pitcher after pitcher, she carried water that slaked the thirst of American soldiers and made it possible for them to continue their fight for freedom.

Molly not only gave water to the weary, but she also was quick to tend to the wounded. On one water trip, she passed a downed soldier who needed help.

17

18

Molly didn't stop to think about her own safety, even though musket balls were whizzing all around her. The soldier needed help. She heaved him onto her back and carried him to a shady place out of harm's way. After she tended his wound, she picked up her pitcher again.

Much to Molly's horror, she saw her husband, William, fall wounded next to his cannon. The rest of the cannon's crew was too exhausted to go on fighting.

Molly didn't dare let the cannon stand idle. She fired it herself.

One by one, the soldiers noticed Molly at the cannon. When they did, they stopped calling, "Molly! Pitcher!" She was a soldier now.

Molly kept that cannon roaring, and the British weren't too happy about it. Some decided to fire back at her. One musket ball came flying low, right at her. Molly spread her legs wide. The ball missed Molly, but it did make quite a hole in her skirt and petticoat.

Molly kept at it, plunging the rammer staff into the cannon again and again. She kept that cannon ringing until the close of battle that day.

As darkness fell, the fighting stopped. It was time to rest and prepare for the next day's fighting.

Back at camp, General Washington asked to meet the able woman he'd noticed firing a cannon in the thick of battle. He told her that for her bravery under heavy fire, she'd earned the rank of sergeant.

The next morning, the American soldiers rallied before dawn. They were ready to pick up the fighting where they'd left off the day before. Sergeant Molly took her post at William's cannon and prepared to fire the big gun. To everyone's surprise, the British had broken camp during the night and sneaked away. The battle was over.

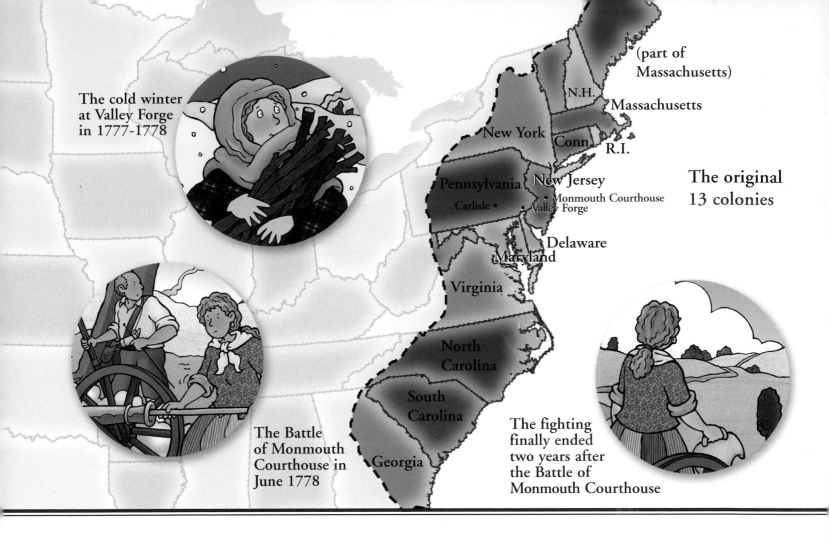

The cold winter at Valley Forge in 1777-1778

The Battle of Monmouth Courthouse in June 1778

The fighting finally ended two years after the Battle of Monmouth Courthouse

The original 13 colonies

(part of Massachusetts)

N.H.

Massachusetts

New York

Conn.

R.I.

Pennsylvania

New Jersey

Carlisle •

• Monmouth Courthouse

• Valley Forge

Delaware

Maryland

Virginia

North Carolina

South Carolina

Georgia

The Real Molly Pitcher

Mary (Molly) Hays McCauley was a real woman. By the time the Revolutionary War fighting ended in 1781, Molly and her husband, William Hays, had settled in Carlisle, Pennsylvania. Molly worked as a cleaning lady and laundress. After William died in 1786, she married John McCauley. In 1822, the Pennsylvania State Legislature voted to give her a pension for her service during the war. Molly McCauley died on January 26, 1832, and is buried in Carlisle, where a monument to her wartime bravery stands at her gravesite.

In honor of Mary Hays McCauley, the United States Field Artillery Association of Fort Sill, Oklahoma, awards a medal to women who exhibit Molly Pitcher's spirit of sacrifice and devotion. The medal is called the Artillery Order of Molly Pitcher.

The source of the story about Molly at the Battle of Monmouth Courthouse is George Washington's step-grandchild, George Washington Parke Custis. He published his memories of his step-grandfather in the late 1820s.

Whether the stories are actually about Molly Hays McCauley remains to be seen. Historians now believe that the contributions of many women during the Revolution combined to create the Molly Pitcher legend.

In any case, the story of Molly Pitcher will always be a tribute to women who are strong, capable, and brave.

Corn Cakes

Soldiers needed a hearty breakfast during the Revolutionary War because their days were long, and they weren't always certain when their next meal would be. Since there was no refrigeration at that time, cooks needed food that could travel well and not spoil. Corn cakes filled the bill on both counts. Here's a recipe that Molly Pitcher was probably familiar with. It's sure to fill the hungriest of soldiers and serves a troop of eight or more.

1 3/4 cups flour
1/4 cup yellow cornmeal
2 teaspoons baking powder
3 teaspoons sugar
1 teaspoon salt

3 eggs
2 cups milk
1/4 cup melted butter, or margarine
1 cup whole kernel corn
(fresh, frozen, or canned)

In a large mixing bowl, combine the dry ingredients. Make a well in the dry ingredients. In another bowl, beat the eggs and milk together. Add the egg-milk mixture to the dry ingredients. Stir in the melted butter. Add the corn and stir lightly.

For each pancake, use about 1/4 cup of the batter. Pour onto a hot griddle or nonstick pan that has been lightly coated with vegetable oil spray. Brown the pancakes on both sides, turning when bubbles appear and the edges are set. Serve with butter and syrup.

Glossary

deserted—left a post in the military without permission

forge—the special furnace in which metal is heated

musket—a gun with a long barrel used before rifles were invented

pension—money paid regularly to people who have retired from work

pewter—a metal made from lead and tin

Prussian—from Prussia, which is now part of Germany

quenched—satisfied or put out

ragamuffins—people in ragged, ill-fitting clothes

ragtag—ragged, sloppy

rammer staff—the rod used to load a charge into a cannon

scores—a score equals a group of 20; a large number

skittish—easily frightened

Did You Know?

➤ "Molly Pitcher" was the name given to many women who carried water to thirsty soldiers during the Revolutionary War.
➤ Mary Hays McCauley, or Molly Pitcher, was not the first woman to take up arms on the battlefields of the Revolutionary War. She was the second one historians know about. The first was named Margaret Corbin. She took her husband's place at the cannon when he was killed by the British at Fort Washington, New York, in 1776.

Want to Know More?

At the Library

Bertanzetti, Eileen Dunn. *Molly Pitcher: Heroine.* Philadelphia: Chelsea House Publishers, 2001.

Ruffin, Frances E. *Molly Pitcher.* New York: PowerKids Press, 2002.

Spies, Karen. *Our Folk Heroes.* Brookfield, Conn.: The Millbrook Press, 1994.

On the Web

For more information on *Molly Pitcher,* use FactHound to track down Web sites related to this book.

1. Go to *www.compasspointbooks.com/ facthound*
2. Type in this book ID: 0756506042
3. Click on the *Fetch It* button.

Your trusty FactHound will fetch the best Web sites for you!

Through the Mail

Valley Forge Convention and Visitors Bureau
600 W. Germantown Pike
Plymouth Meeting, PA 19462
To get information about visiting the Valley Forge area

Cumberland County Historical Society
21 N. Pitt St.
Carlisle, PA 17013
info@historicalsociety.com
To get information about Mary Hays McCauley

On the Road

Monmouth Battlefield State Park
347 Freehold-Englishtown Road
Manalapan, NJ 07726
732/462-9616
To tour the site of the Battle of Monmouth Courthouse and learn more about the Revolutionary War

Index

About the Author

Larry Dane Brimner has written more than 100 books for young people, including the award-winning *Merry Christmas, Old Armadillo* (Boyds Mills Press) and *The Littlest Wolf* (HarperCollins Publishers). He is also the reteller of several other Tall Tales, including *Calamity Jane, Casey Jones, Captain Stormalong,* and *Davy Crockett.* Mr. Brimner lives in the historic Old Pueblo (Tucson, Arizona).

About the Illustrator

Patrick Girouard has been drawing and painting for many years. He has illustrated more than 50 books for children, including *Paul Bunyan* in this series. Patrick has two sons, Marc and Max, and a dog called Sam. They all live in Indiana.